W9-AGG-018

Copyright© 2000 by Thomas O'Neal Davison

All rights reserved. No part of this book may be reproduced or transmitted in any form or by any means, electronic or mechanical, including photocopying, recording, or by any information storage and retrieval system, without permission in writing from the author.

Printed in the United States

Published by Thomas O'Neal Davison
P.O. Box 130694
Roseville, MN 55113-0006

Book layout, typeset and cover design by Associates by Design
Cover illustration by Samuel J. Simmons

ISBN: 0-9679028-0-0

Daddy, Can You Hear Me?

Written By

Thomas O'Neal Davison

Illustrated By

Samuel J. Simmons

Devotional

This book is dedicated to the memory of Mr. O'Neal Davison who was not only "My Daddy," but my friend and hero. Also, a very special dedication to all those outstanding people who find themselves in the role of both "Mommy and Daddy."

Important preface

This book orchestrates alternating feelings and thoughts between child and father. The child's feelings and thoughts are in blue type.

Daddy, can you hear me?

I'm just a moment away!

Daddy, can you hear me calling out your name?
Even though I don't remember seeing your face,
people say I look just like you. . .
Is that true?
I really hope I do!

Close your eyes and think. . .
about all the times you wished I were there. . .
Believe me, in spirit I was there!
My love for you. . .
always allows me to be. . .
just a moment away!

I have spent so many days. . .
and so many nights, thinking of you.
I wonder if you know. . .
I am your number one fan!
Really I am!

Countless days and countless nights. . .
all filled with thoughts of you.
Thinking of you always makes me smile.
I know that you are being the best. . .
you can be, without me.

We have laughed together, cried together. . .
slept together, eaten together. . .
played together, stayed together. . .
Each and every night. . .
we pray together. . .
all in my mind.

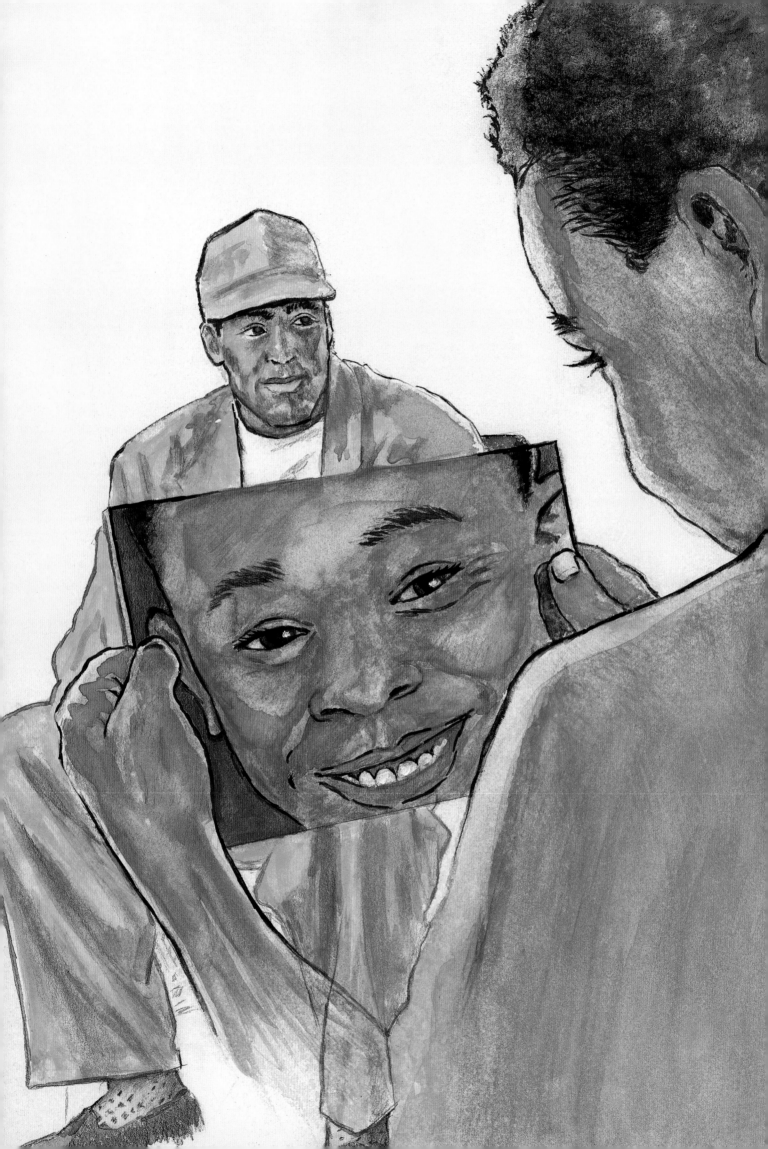

Find a mirror and look deep inside yourself.
Look deep and you will see. . .
my love for you.
It's locked inside your secret closet
just waiting to hold you
in its comforting arms.

You taught me how to ride a bike,
how to catch, how to throw,
how to bait a hook and fish,
how to play hide and seek.
You even taught me how to be cool.
All of this in my dreams.

I can't explain my absence,
but life is not always
a fair game to play.
But always remember, never forget
you are truly, the sunshine of my life,
because you are the best part of me!

We've been to the park, to the lake,
to the zoo, to the movies,
to the mall, to the pizza place.
You've even taken me to grandma's house!
Oh what fun I have
daydreaming of you!

You must wonder where I am?
Though I don't really know how to explain,
remember my love is with you always.
Don't forget we will always
be a part of each other. . .
Just a moment away!

You took me for a ride in your brand new car,
we were so cool in our sunglasses.
We stopped for ice cream
and both had chocolate.
We are so much alike,
best of friends!

My favorite songs remind me of you,
"The Greatest Love of All" and . . .
"I Will Always Love You". . .
just to name a few.
You are a very special person,
one-of-a-kind
just like me!

Daddy, I need you when
I go to the doctor, to the dentist
and to the principal's office.
Sometimes I am so scared
it really helps to take you with me,
inside my mind.

So many times, I wished things to be different.
As you grow,
I want you to be able to smile
knowing my love for you
is always and forever
a moment away!

Daddy, you're always a part of my Thanksgiving,
my Christmas, and my birthday.
I need you most on Halloween.
I feel so safe
when we're together.
We are a great team
you and me!

*The gift of love will one day
bring us together, face to face.
I hope to be ready to meet
such an important person, you!
Until then, whatever you do
don't you ever forget. . .*

I want you to know my friends;
I also want to know yours.
You have made me proud, so many times
just knowing I belong to you!
You are forever in my heart.

*Each and every day, I pray for you;
and each and every day, I think of you.
Although I'm not there, I still have
something to say. My love for you
allows me to be just a moment away
I L-O-V-E YOU!*

Daddy, can you hear me?
I've enjoyed my time thinking about you.
Do dreams really come true?
I'll know if I ever see you, they do!
I pray every night that I'll see you soon.
Good night.